MW00903192

Prater the Prairie Dog

Dave and Pat Sargent are longtime residents of Prairie Grove, Arkansas. Dave, a fourth-generation dairy farmer, began writing in early December 1990, and Pat, a former teacher, began writing shortly after. They enjoy the outdoors and have a real love for animals.

Prater the Prairie Dog

By

Dave and Pat Sargent

Illustrated by
Jeane Huff

Ozark Publishing, Inc.
P.O. Box 228
Prairie Grove, AR 72753

Library of Congress cataloging-in-publication data

Sargent, Dave, 1941—
    Prater the prairie dog / by Dave and Pat Sargent ;
illustrated by Jeane Huff.
    p. cm.
    Summary: Prater worries about a lot of things, but he
  fails to be concerned about the big bald eagle soaring
  around above him looking for a nice little dinner.
    ISBN 1-56763-384-6 (cb). — ISBN 1-56763-385-
  4 (pb)
    [1. Prairie dogs—Fiction. 2. Behvior—Fiction.]
I. Sargent, Pat, 1936— .
    II. Huff, Jeane, 1946— ill. III. Title.
    PZ7.S2465Pr 1998   97-27203
    [E]—dc21   CIP
                                         AC

Printed in the United States of America

iv

Inspired by

watching little prairie dogs pop in and out of their holes, playing.

Dedicated to

all children who live in the country
and enjoy watching prairie dogs at
play, popping in and out of their
mounds.

Foreword

Prater is a young prairie dog who is a worrywart. Ole Baldy's sharp talons grab Prater, and he is almost carried away. Just in time, Barney the Bear Killer spots the eagle and guesses his intentions. Just as little Prater is being lifted into the air, Barney lunges. He grabs a mouthful of tail feathers and hangs on tight.

Contents

ix

Prater the Prairie Dog

If you would like to have the authors of the Animal Pride Series visit your school, free of charge, call 1-800-321-5671 or 1-800-960-3876.

One

The Bald Eagle

Prater lay there naked and blind in a grass-lined nest in a side burrow of the tunnel. He lay curled up and piled up with his two brothers and two sisters.

When prairie dogs are born, they have no fur, and their eyes do not open for a couple of weeks. Prater wasn't very old and was already becoming a worrywart; at least, that's what his mama called him. He asked a million questions a day and worried about everything.

One day, Prater noticed that his brothers and sisters had yellowish-brown fur, and he didn't have any. He was still as naked as a jaybird, as the saying goes. He kept asking his mama the same question over and over. He asked, "Why, Mama? Why don't I have fur like everyone else?"

Mama Prairie Dog could only shrug her shoulders and shake her head as she'd answer, "I don't know, Prater. I really don't know."

So, Prater kept worrying. Why was he different? Would he never grow fur? Would he never look like his brothers and sisters? What was wrong with him, anyway? Why did he have to be different?

Prater and his family lived in a prairie dog town, which contained hundreds of prairie dogs.

Little Prater and his brothers and sisters would stay in the burrow for two years; then they would have to make burrows of their own.

"Prater, wake up!" Mama called one morning. "Guess what, Prater. You have fur! I can see a little fuzzy brown fur growing on your back and on your little head. Isn't this great, Prater? Now, you can stop worrying, 'cause you're not bald anymore! And you can stop bugging me about not having any fur!"

Prater jumped out of bed. He ran to the entrance of the burrow so he could see better. Sure enough, as he turned to look over his shoulder, he saw a fuzzy film of yellowish-brown fur on his back. And when he looked at the rest of his body, he saw the same thing!

At the entrance to each burrow sat a sentinel. The sentinels were the prairie dogs on guard, ready to sound an alarm in case of danger.

Suddenly, right behind Prater, the sentinel at Prater's burrow sounded an alarm. And soon, the other sentinels joined in. Short yaps could be heard at the entrance of each burrow.

Little Prater stood on his back legs and looked all around. He saw an animal in the distance. What he didn't see was the big bald eagle soaring high above him. He was surprised when the sentinels started popping into their holes. Wow! He was alone! All five inches of him.

Prater felt very important. And look at all the space he could play in. Why, he had the entire field to himself, the whole world maybe.

Two

Prater Can Fly!

Barney the Bear Killer was out making his early morning rounds through the edge of the woods, the pasture where the dry cows were kept, the maternity pasture where the new baby calves were born, and, in general, the entire farm. He felt it was his responsibility to keep out all intruders. And he did a good job of it, too.

Now, Barney was aware of ole Baldy's presence on the dairy farm. Baldy's nest was on top of the high mountain that stood on the back side of Farmer John's place. It was Baldy's job to help clean up the farms in the area, like keeping them free of any remains of dead animals that had not been disposed of by small, meat-eating animals.

When Baldy began circling over little Prater, much like buzzards circle, Barney's eyes searched the ground under Baldy. And sure enough, there sat Prater looking around. Barney knew the little prairie dog would be a goner if he didn't get to him before the eagle swooped down. Yes siree, that little prairie dog would be Baldy's supper.

Prater's body was shaking as he jerked his head in all directions. Something was wrong. He sensed it. What could it be that was making him so nervous? It must be that big ole black and tan animal that was headed his way, because now that animal was running fast. And he was coming straight for Prater.

Prater was standing close to the burrow entrance. He was right on top of the three-foot-high mound of dirt that encircled it. Suddenly, he heard a swooshing sound. And then he heard a bay coming from that big animal that had almost reached him. Oh, no! Things were happening too fast! What was he supposed to do?

Barney the Bear Killer knew he should rescue the little prairie dog if he could, because the prairie dogs belonged on Farmer John's place. They had lived there a lot longer than Barney. He picked up speed.

Mama Prairie Dog ran past the sentinel that had popped into the hole. She reached out and grabbed the very tip of Prater's one-inch tail. She tried to hold on, but with Prater shaking from being so scared, her

grip slipped, and Prater tumbled
down the outside of the three-foot
mound of dirt. Oh, no! Poor Prater!

Little Prater sensed something hovering over him. Then, long, hooked talons dug into his back. He felt himself being lifted into the air.

Barney the Bear Killer made a leap. He jumped about as high as he had ever jumped before. He grabbed a mouthful of tail feathers and held on tight, not knowing for sure if Baldy was strong enough to lift him and Prater into the air—he hoped not.

Mama Prairie Dog was jumping up and down, crying, "Come back! Come back with my baby! He's so little! He's my little Prater, my little worrywart! Come back!"

Prater was scared. He wanted his mama. He heard her calling his name.

Barney the Bear Killer felt Baldy level off; then, much to his relief, he felt himself coming back down. His ninety-five pounds was too much for Baldy to carry. Good! Barney felt his back feet touch the ground, but he wouldn't let go of his mouthful of tail feathers, not until he knew the little prairie dog was safe.

When Barney's four feet were on solid ground, he dug in. He tried holding the eagle down, but it was no use. That big bald eagle would not quit flapping his wings. He was determined to take off again.

Baldy wanted Barney to turn loose of his tail, so Baldy let go of Prater. Prater hit the ground with a thud. He rolled and tumbled, head over heels, until he finally stopped at the edge of a great big pond.

Now, Prater had always been a worrywart. If he wasn't worrying about something, he was worrying his mama. Well, now Prater really had done something to cause his mama to worry. He had done what she had told him he should never do. He had gone outside alone. He knew his mama was probably worried about him right now.

Prater wanted to go home and tell his mama that he was all right. But when he looked all around, he didn't see anything familiar. And when he stuck his nose in the air to see if he could pick up a familiar scent, he couldn't smell a thing. You see, Prater had bumped his nose when he had fallen, and it was swollen shut.

Three

The Clover Cluster Hideout

Mama Prairie Dog was running back and forth outside the burrow, looking for Prater. He was nowhere to be seen. "Oh, my!" she cried. "Even when my little Prater isn't here, he worries me. By now, he's probably inside that bald eagle's stomach. I just know that bald eagle has already eaten him!"

Barney had let go of Baldy's tail feathers when he saw Baldy let go of Prater. And since Barney was only two or three feet off the ground, he didn't have far to fall. He stood and watched Baldy. The eagle was climbing now, heading for his nest on top of the mountain.

Barney immediately began searching for the little prairie dog. The only problem was that the prairie dog was so small. He would be hard to find in the tall grass. But Barney wanted to try. He knew the little thing would never find his way back home alone. So Barney put his nose to the ground, trying to pick up Prater's scent.

Prater heard Barney coming. He wasn't hearing ole Barney's feet hitting the grass-covered ground, but rather Barney's long nose going "sniff, sniff, sniff."

Prater knew Barney had saved him, but he didn't know whether Barney had saved him because he was nice and wanted to be his friend, or if he had saved him from the eagle so he could eat him himself. Little Prater didn't know what to do. He finally decided to hide under a big cluster of clover.

Lucky for Prater, ole Barney was used to tracking raccoons and other animals. And like any good coonhound would, he ended up at Prater's hiding place. Barney circled the cluster of clover, then stopped and lay down.

Prater's heart was racing. It was running faster than Prater's legs ever could. What was he supposed to do now? He peeked out between the clover blooms and saw two big eyes, two long ears, a long black nose, a big mouth with a red tongue hanging out, and millions of long sharp teeth!

Barney whined a low whine, and little Prater thought, "He doesn't sound so mean. Maybe he wants to be my friend." And with that thought in mind, Prater crawled out from under the big cluster of clover. Barney the Bear Killer stood up.

When Prater looked up, all he could see were Barney's feet. He leaned his head back, and there, way up in the air, was that big face with the long, sharp teeth. Boy! Prater's heart stopped beating almost.

Barney sniffed Prater up and down and all around. Again, he whined a low whine and did that funny grin of his. Prater decided that Barney wanted to be friends.

Barney's teeth grasped Prater by the nape of his neck. At first, he lifted the little prairie dog only about a foot off the ground, just to see if Prater would be scared. Barney hoped Prater would stay calm and not jerk away, because too much movement would tear Prater's hide right off his skinny little body.

When Barney was sure that Prater was okay about being carried by the nape of the neck, he started in the direction of prairie dog town. And while he was being carried, Prater kept his eyes closed tight.

Finally, there in the distance lay prairie dog town. Barney could see Mama Prairie Dog running back and forth and all around, looking for Prater. He heard her calling, "Prater! Where are you, son? Come home, Prater! Mama misses you!"

When Prater heard his mama calling, he opened his eyes and looked for his mama. Despite the swaying ride he was getting with ole Barney carrying him, he could make out his mama's shape.

When Barney got closer, he sat Prater on the ground, then stood still, waiting to see what the little thing would do.

Prater Prairie Dog ran toward his mama, then stopped and looked back at Barney. He chattered something, and his skinny body did a funny little twist. He seemed to be telling Barney, "Thanks, Barney. Thanks for saving my life."

Mama Prairie Dog had caught sight of Prater, just as he turned back to look at the coonhound. She, too, understood what Prater was saying. She ran to Prater and nudged him over and over with her nose.

Mama Prairie Dog was glad to see her little Prater. She was glad her little worrywart was safely home.

Four

Prairie Dog Facts

The prairie dog's official name is *Cynomys ludovicianus.* No one uses this scientific name.

The prairie dog is not a dog, but a stout, short-legged, burrowing squirrel. It lives on the plains and plateaus from the Canadian border south to Mexico.

The prairie dog is about eleven to thirteen inches long and has a four-inch tail. The fur is yellowish-brown above and buff tinged with brown below.

Prairie dogs live in colonies or "towns," containing thousands of individuals. A town is organized into wards along topographic lines. Each ward contains several, sometimes hundreds, of coteries, each headed by a male who has won his place by fighting. His entourage consists of one to four females and the young of the past two years.

The individual burrows are very complex. A mound of dirt two or

three feet high completely encircles
the entrance to keep out surface
water. Here the prairie dog sits
upright as a sentinel.

If dangers appears, the sentinel sounds the alarm, a sort of sharp "yap"—hence the name prairie dog. There are several alarm calls, depending on the type of threat. If there is real danger the prairie dog pops into its hole.

The prairie dog may live to be ten years old. In the spring, the female bears a litter of five naked, blind young in a grass-lined nest in a side burrow of the tunnel.